Frankie's MAGIC SOCCER BALL

FRANKIE VS. THE MUMMY'S MENACE

ALSO BY FRANK LAMPARD

FRANKIE VS. THE MUMMY'S MENACE

FRANK LAMPARD

SCHOLASTIC INC.

No part of this publication may be reproduced, stored in a retrieval system, or transmitted in any form or by any means, electronic, mechanical, photocopying, recording, or otherwise, without written permission of the publisher. For information regarding permission, write to Little, Brown Book Group, 100 Victoria Embankment, London EC4Y ODY, United Kingdom.

ISBN 978-0-545-66618-3

Published by Scholastic Inc., 557 Broadway, New York, NY 10012, by arrangement with Little, Brown Books for Young Readers. SCHOLASTIC and associated logos are trademarks and/or registered trademarks of Scholastic Inc.

12 11 10 9 8 7 6 5 4 3 2 1   14 15 16 17 18 19/0

Printed in the U.S.A.   40
First printing, August 2014

To my mom, Pat,
who encouraged me to do my
homework in between kicking a ball
all around the house, and is still
with me every step of the way.

Welcome to a fantastic
fantasy league — the greatest
soccer competition ever held in
this world or any other!

You'll need four on a team,
so choose carefully. This is a lot
more serious than a game in the
park. You'll never know who your
next opponents will be, or where
you'll face them.

So lace up your cleats, players,
and good luck! The whistle's
about to blow!

The Ref

CHAPTER 1

Frankie stood in front of the marble statue. He checked the question on his handout.

"Who ruled the Roman Empire in 60 AD?"

He read the little card on the wall.

THE EMPEROR NERO (RULED 54–68 AD)

Wow! he thought. *That's nearly two thousand years ago!*

He wrote the answer: Nero.

Frankie heard the shuffle of footsteps and turned to see his friend Charlie dragging his feet. He was carrying his clipboard in his hands.

"This museum is the most boring place in the universe," said Charlie.

"More boring than math class with Ms. Brown?" asked Frankie, grinning.

"Okay, the *second* most boring place," said Charlie. "I can't believe they canceled soccer practice for this." He flopped onto the bottom step of the staircase, tossed the clipboard aside, and rested his chin in his gloved hands. Frankie saw Charlie had filled in some of the answers, but not many.

"Ahem!" said a voice. Mr. Donald strode out from behind another statue. "Charles, I don't see how you're going to complete your assignment unless you take those goalkeeping gloves off."

Frankie saw his friend quickly hide his clipboard. "I answered all the questions," said Charlie.

"Oh, really?" asked Mr. Donald, narrowing his eyes. "I don't see how that's possible. You haven't even visited the Egyptian gallery yet and we have to leave in fifteen minutes."

Charlie blushed. "Just going now," he said. With a sigh he stood up and began to climb the stairs.

"Wait for me," said Frankie. "I'm finished with the Roman questions."

"Good job," said Mr. Donald. "Your friend Louise is already up there. Almost done, I believe."

"She would be!" grumbled Charlie.

As they followed the sign to the Egyptian gallery, they passed the café. Loud shouts and laughter came from inside. A moment later, Frankie's brother, Kevin, and his friends spilled

4

out. When his eyes landed on Frankie, he stopped laughing and sneered.

"It's the Dork Squad!" he said. "Have you answered all of Donaldo's questions yet?"

"Just keep walking," Frankie whispered to Charlie. He'd hoped he wouldn't bump into his brother's class. They were at the museum, too, researching their own history projects.

Frankie and Charlie found Louise in the Egyptian room inspecting a green jar on a glass shelf. "This belonged to a pharaoh," she said when she spotted them.

"A fair–what?" asked Charlie.

Louise rolled her eyes. "'Pharaoh' was the name ancient Egyptians gave their king," she said.

"Yeah, I knew that," mumbled Charlie.

"They used this jar to store the heart after the pharaoh was mummified," said Louise.

"Yuck!" said Frankie. He checked his handout. "We have to find the names of five Egyptian gods," he added. "Apparently the Egyptians worshipped more than sixty!"

"I've got four already," said Louise. She grinned and hid her answer sheet as Charlie peered over her shoulder. "Don't copy me!"

Frankie wasn't interested in Louise's answers. He was looking at something in the center of the room, separated by a red rope. It was like an open coffin standing on its end. The lid was decorated with the face and body of a man. He wore a colorful headdress, painted gold and red, and he had a strange, thin beard. Across his clothes were hundreds of tiny symbols.

"Check that out," Frankie said.

"That's the mummy's sarcophagus," said Louise.

"Sark–off–a–what?" asked Charlie.

"Like a coffin," said Louise. "When a pharaoh died, his body was preserved as a mummy, then the mummy was put inside a sarcophagus, and then in a pyramid."

Frankie marveled at the amazing painted details.

The card next to the exhibit read:

SARCOPHAGUS OF UNKNOWN PHARAOH.

"I wonder what all the little pictures mean," said Charlie.

"They're called hieroglyphs," said Louise.

"Hire–oh–what?" said Charlie, smiling. "Only kidding."

Frankie peered even closer, right into the golden eyes of the unknown pharaoh. Then he felt his bag strap pull on his shoulder, almost dragging him off his feet. He spun around to see Kevin grabbing his bag.

"Hey! I'm not finished with you, little brother."

"Give that back!" yelled Frankie.

"Ooh . . . scary!" said his brother. He unzipped Frankie's bag and tipped it upside down. Out fell Frankie's pencil case, his lunchbox, and his books. And, last of all, his battered soccer ball. He dropped the bag at Frankie's feet.

"Pass it here!" said Kevin's friend Liam.

Before Frankie could react, Kevin backheeled the ball to Liam.

"Don't do that!" said Louise. "You'll break something!"

"What are you scared of?" asked Kevin's friend Matt. "The mummy's curse?"

Charlie went to get the ball, but Liam chipped it over his shoulder to Rob. All Kevin's friends were laughing. Frankie stuffed his things into his bag and sprang to his feet.

"Come and get your ball," said Rob, stepping over it.

Frankie ran at him, his blood pumping. Rob tried to go around him, but Frankie kept his eye on the ball and tackled him. The ball spun up into the air, straight toward the ancient green jar.

Frankie, and everyone else, sucked in a breath.

The ball just missed the jar and rolled under the rope, toward the mummy's sarcophagus.

"What are you kids up to?" said a voice over the silence. It was Mrs. Murray, Kevin's history teacher. She might only have been five feet tall and about a hundred years old, but Frankie knew they were terrified

of her. "Don't you have work to do?" she said.

Kevin and his friends all scattered quickly, muttering "Yes, Mrs. Murray" and "Sorry."

Mrs. Murray glared at Frankie, then followed them out of the room.

"Whew!" said Louise. "That jar is priceless!"

Frankie blew out a long breath and went to get his ball. He stopped right in his tracks when he saw the ball had somehow rolled *inside* the sarcophagus. "Weird," he said.

"What?" asked Charlie.

Frankie pointed over at the sarcophagus. "Did you put it in there?"

Both Louise and Charlie shook their heads.

Frankie edged closer. He was going to have to step over the rope to get the ball. He looked up, checking for cameras. *If Mr. Donald sees me, I'm going to be in deep trouble.*

As he lifted a leg over the rope, the painted gold eyes of the pharaoh watched him intently. Frankie didn't believe in a mummy's curse, but he couldn't help shuddering.

He reached out for the ball, heart thumping.

Then, with no one touching it, the sarcophagus lid snapped shut.

CHAPTER 2

Louise squealed and Frankie jerked his hand back.

"Is it supposed to do that?" Charlie asked. His skin was pale.

"The wind must have blown it shut," said Frankie. "Help me get it open again."

"I'll keep lookout," said Louise.

She went to stand by the door as Charlie jumped over the rope to Frankie's side. They each gripped the crack of the coffin lid and pulled. With a blast of hot air, they managed to pull it open.

"Not again!" Charlie groaned.

Frankie found a smile playing over his lips. There was no sign of the soccer ball in the sarcophagus, but instead there was a colorful, swirling doorway.

"Time for another adventure," said Frankie.

Charlie frowned. "I'm not sure this time."

From her lookout position, Louise

gasped. "Donaldo's coming! Quick!"
She rushed over and hurled herself
through the portal.

"Are you coming?" said Frankie.

"I guess I haven't got a choice any
more," said Charlie. He leapt through
after Louise.

"Where did you guys go?" called
Mr. Donald. "The bus will be leaving
in five minutes."

Frankie saw his teacher's shadow
approaching down the corridor.

"Now or never," he muttered and
stepped into the sarcophagus.

"Aaah!" Frankie was falling,
tumbling over and over. Something
gritty filled his mouth, drowning his

cries. The world was a blur. He couldn't see because his eyes were blinking hard.

He rolled onto his back.

Frankie opened his eyes and saw the sun like a golden disc right overhead. The sky was the purest blue he'd ever seen, without a cloud in sight. He felt sand in his fingers.

"Where are we?" said Charlie.

Frankie sat up and saw an enormous sand dune rising above him.

"We're in the desert," he said, climbing to his feet and brushing off his clothes.

Only they weren't his clothes. Like Charlie, he was wearing a linen tunic,

21

tied at the waist with a belt. Louise wore a blue dress that fell all the way to her ankles.

Frankie turned around, but all he could see was more sand, stretching for miles.

"The magic soccer ball must have brought us here to play a game," he said.

Charlie spat out a mouthful of sand and shielded his eyes from the sun with a glove. "Maybe it's broken," he said, "because we're in the middle of nowhere."

"And we don't have any water," said Louise. She looked down and yelped. "What's that?"

The sand by her feet was moving. Something was squirming around beneath the surface. A furry snout broke loose, followed by a dog's head.

"Max!" cried Frankie.

"Don't just stand there!" barked the little dog. "Help a hound out, why don't you?"

Frankie fell to his knees and started scooping sand away. Soon Max scrambled free and shook the sand out of his fur.

"Great," he said. "I was having a nice snooze by the back door."

"The magic soccer ball must have brought you," said Frankie, "even though you weren't with us in the museum."

"Brought me where, exactly?" asked Max.

Frankie shrugged. He set off up the side of the sand dune with the sun beating down on his head. The others followed after him, slipping and sliding on the loose sand.

As Frankie reached the crest of the dune, he gasped. In the distance, rising out of the desert, was an enormous pyramid. It blurred in the haze of heat rising from the ground.

"We're in ancient Egypt!" said Louise.

"But where are our opponents?"
asked Charlie.

Frankie pointed to the pyramid.
"My guess is we'll find them over
there. Let's go!"

They trudged down the other side
of the dune toward the pyramid.

"It's bigger than I ever imagined," said Louise. "Did you know that the pyramids sometimes took more than twenty years to build? They had to drag the huge blocks of stone from the Nile River by hand. Some pyramids had over a million blocks."

"Whoa!" said Charlie. "That would be even more boring than math homework."

Max was having trouble keeping up because his paws kept sinking in the sand. Frankie stooped to pick him up. As he rose again, he saw a cart approaching, drawn by a camel.

The driver drew up alongside them and Frankie saw the cart was empty.

"What are you doing out here, wandering in the desert heat?" asked the man.

Frankie searched his mind for an answer, and decided on the truth.

"We're here for a game of soccer," he said.

"Aren't we all?" said the man, settling back onto a large cushion. "Who are you rooting for?"

"We're playing, actually," said Frankie.

"We're Frankie's Fantasy FC," added Louise.

The man looked at them solemnly for a moment, and then burst out laughing.

"Very funny!" he said. "You almost had me there!"

"We're serious," said Charlie, holding up his hands. "Why do you think I'm wearing these?"

The man was serious again. "I'm not sure why you're wearing gloves in the desert," he said. "But a bunch of kids haven't got a snowball's chance in the desert of beating King Tut's team."

CHAPTER 3

Frankie looked at his friends. "Don't worry," he said. "We've played against plenty of tough opponents." But even he was secretly worried. "Can you take us to the pyramid?" he asked.

The man grinned. "Of course!" he said. "The name's Medhi. Hop on."

In a short while, they reached the side of the pyramid. Up close, it seemed even bigger, completely blocking out the sun in the sky. Hundreds of people were gathered near a doorway, where two bare-chested guards with swords hanging at their sides were letting them in a few at a time.

"Where are they going?" asked Charlie. "Is it hollow?"

Louise shook her head. "No, but there are chambers and secret passageways inside."

"Cool!" said Frankie.

"You'd better get out here while I

find somewhere to park my camel," said Medhi. "Join the line."

Frankie and his friends jumped out. The camel drew back its lips and hissed when it saw Max near its ankles.

"Don't mind her," Medhi said. "She's more of a cat lover. Doesn't like stray dogs."

"I'm no stray!" said Max. "I'm a house dog, thank you very much."

They walked over to the spectators waiting to get in. There were men and women, young and old. Some sheltered under parasols, while others wafted their faces with fans.

"We need to get inside and find the referee," said Frankie. He tapped a man on the shoulder. "Excuse me, can we get in, please?"

"No," said the man. "Wait your turn."

Frankie noticed that many of the people lining up were clutching rough pieces of paper, showing a line drawing of a man standing over a soccer ball. Frankie remembered from the museum that the Egyptians wrote on something called papyrus — paper made from river reeds.

"Any idea who the opponents are today?" asked a woman with an elaborate hairstyle pinned up on her head.

"Nope," said a thin man, sipping from a water flask. "Who cares? They'll lose like all the others, and end up locked in the pyramid for eternity."

Charlie's eyes went wide. "Hang on. Isn't eternity a long time?"

"It's *forever*," said Louise.

"We're not going to lose," said Frankie. He looked around for Medhi, but he'd vanished.

At that moment, shouts went up at the back of the crowd and another guard came rushing through. He

shouted, "Move! Make way for King Tut!"

A murmur passed through the crowd and everyone shuffled aside. A row of servants approached, carrying a kind of couch on their shoulders. On top of the couch was a boy a bit older than Frankie, his chin raised proudly. Beside him sat a girl. They looked so alike that they had to be brother and sister. The servants carried them inside.

Eventually Frankie and his friends reached the front of the line.

"Tickets, please," said a bare-chested guard.

Frankie looked at Louise, but she just shrugged. "We don't have tickets," he said.

The guard folded his beefy arms and glowered. "No tickets, no entry," he said.

"But we're here to play!" said Charlie.

The guard looked Charlie up and

down. Then he started laughing and gave his fellow guard a friendly slap on the shoulder. "Yes, and my brother is the god Anubis!" he said, tears pouring down his face.

"Hey!" said a woman's voice. "Where's my bracelet?"

Everyone, including Frankie, turned. The woman was feeling her wrist, frowning.

"And my ring's gone, too!" said the man next to her. He narrowed his eyes. "There's a pickpocket around here."

His eyes settled on Frankie and his friends. So did everyone else's.

"It wasn't us . . ." said Louise.

Frankie heard the hiss of metal as the guards drew their swords.

"Run!" he shouted.

They dashed out of the line as the crowd erupted in shouting. Frankie didn't know which way to go, so he headed alongside the pyramid until his breath was coming hard and fast and his legs were aching. When he looked back, he saw that no one was following them.

Charlie had his hands on his knees, panting.

Max kicked up some sand. "It's like being at the beach, but there are no crabs to chase."

Frankie was wondering what to do next when Louise pointed past him. "Isn't that Medhi?" she said.

Frankie saw him, too. Medhi was standing at the base of the pyramid, running his fingers along the blocks as if he was looking for something.

"Hey!" said Frankie.

Medhi straightened up, blushing as they approached.

"You don't have a ticket, either?" asked Charlie.

"Something like that." Medhi grinned.

"What are you doing?" asked Louise.

Medhi's grin stayed fixed. "Oh, you know, just sightseeing." He waved a hand at the surrounding area. As he did so, Frankie saw a flash of gold on his wrist. It was a bracelet he was sure Medhi hadn't been wearing before. Come to think of it, there was a silver ring on his finger, too.

"You're the thief!" gasped Frankie.

"He's a tomb robber, I'll bet," said Louise. "Looking to steal the pharaoh's treasure."

Medhi raised his finger to his lips. "Shhh! Anyway, what proof have you got?"

Max growled. "Maybe we should summon those guards with the sharp swords."

Medhi spread his hands. "No need for that, fellow travelers. Can't we make a deal?" He took the bracelet off his wrist and held it out to Louise.

Frankie was about to call the guards when he had a better idea.

"Maybe we *can* make a deal," he said.

He saw Louise's eyes grow wide. "But he's a crook!" she said.

"Help us get inside the pyramid," said Frankie, "and we won't tell on you."

Charlie smiled. "Good thinking, Captain," he said.

Medhi stroked his chin and then nodded. "All right. I know there's a loose block here somewhere leading to a secret passage. We just have to find it."

Frankie gazed at the huge pyramid. "There must be thousands of stones!" he said.

But Max was already scampering through the sand, nose to the blocks. About halfway along, he paused. "Over here!" he barked.

Frankie and the others rushed over, including Medhi. Max rested his paws on the stone.

"How do you know it's that one?" asked the pickpocket.

"I can smell the air on the other side," said Max. "Not such a useless stray, after all?"

Frankie and Louise set their shoulders against one side of the block. They strained against the stone, but it didn't budge.

"Are you sure?" Frankie asked Max.

"Come on, you weaklings," said the dog.

Charlie pressed both gloves against the block and joined the effort.

"You too!" said Frankie to Medhi.

The robber laid his back against the block.

"On three," said Frankie. "One . . . two . . . three!"

They all grunted and pushed. With a grinding sound, the rock slid into the pyramid, revealing a black passage beyond.

"We're in!" said Frankie.

CHAPTER 4

"You guys are naturals," said Medhi, rushing back and grabbing a sack from the sand.

"We're not thieves like you," said Louise as she crept into the darkness. Frankie followed her, with Max at his heels.

"Wait until you see the mummy's mask!" said Medhi, heading in last. "It's solid gold and worth a fortune! You'll soon forget about soccer."

With only the sunlight from outside trickling into the passage, it was gloomy. But when Frankie's eyes began to adjust, he made out smooth carved walls and a tunnel leading deep into the pyramid.

"Be careful," said Louise. "My library book told me that the people who made the pyramids often set booby traps to stop tomb robbers."

"I don't like the sound of that," said Charlie.

"They just say that to scare us off," said Medhi. "It's perfectly safe."

Frankie heard a scurrying sound ahead. "Is that you, Max?" he asked.

"Nope," said his dog.

"I don't like the sound of it, either!" whispered Charlie.

"Just relax," said Medhi. "It's just scarab beetles, and maybe the odd scorpion."

"And that's supposed to make us relax?" said Max. "No wonder you're following up at the rear."

Frankie heard a faint *click*, then . . . WHOOSH!

A shape shot through the darkness straight toward Max, who froze.

Charlie dove and stretched out an arm. The object rebounded into a wall with a crash. As the dust cleared, Frankie saw it was a stone soccer ball.

"Nobody move!" said Frankie.

No more balls came whizzing through the air. Frankie slowly crouched by Max's side. "Lift your

paws one at a time," he said. As Max obeyed, Frankie saw a stone button under his left front paw, almost hidden under a coating of sand.

"Our first booby trap," said Frankie.

"Let's go back," said Charlie. "It's too dangerous."

As he turned, Medhi blocked his way, raising a pickax threateningly. "I don't think so," he said. "We're going to find that mask or die trying."

"I knew we shouldn't have trusted you," said Louise.

Frankie's anger swelled, but he tried to keep a clear head. He looked at the stone ball that had almost squished Max. There could have been dozens of them hidden away, ready to shoot out.

"I've got an idea!" he said. He reached over and picked up the heavy ball.

Just what I need, he thought.

"Move it!" said the robber.

Frankie faced the empty corridor, then drew back his arm like he was at the bowling alley. He sent the ball rolling straight down the center of the passageway.

Click . . . click . . . clickety . . . click . . .

As the stone soccer ball bobbled over more hidden switches, stones shot from the walls like cannonballs. Some thumped into the ground, while others rebounded off the walls. Some collided and smashed each other to dust.

Slowly the cloud of debris settled.

"Good thinking!" said Charlie. "You set off all the traps."

Frankie breathed a sigh of relief. "Let's go," he said.

They set off through the rubble, making sure they walked exactly where the ball had rolled.

"So who else is on King Tut's

team?" said Louise. "We only saw him with a girl."

"That's his sister, Princess Cleo," said Medhi. "The captain is King Tut's dad . . . the Menacing Mummy."

"A mummy?" asked Louise. "You mean, like a dead person wrapped in bandages?"

"Careful what you say," said Medhi. "He's very proud. King Tut's dad was a huge soccer fan. He made sure that Tut practiced every day."

"Who's the fourth player?" asked Charlie.

Medhi grinned uneasily. "You probably don't want to know."

The passage became darker and darker, until soon Frankie could see barely five paces ahead. "At least there are no more flying soccer balls," muttered Max.

They heard a deep rumble.

"What's that?" said Medhi.

The rumbling grew louder, like approaching thunder.

"Uh-oh!" said Charlie, looking back.

Frankie glanced back, too. A huge shadow was rolling toward them — a stone soccer ball as big as a car that completely filled the tunnel.

Medhi dropped his pickax and pushed Louise out of the way. He

took off down the passage at top speed.

"I don't think I can save *that*!" said Charlie.

"Run!" said Frankie.

Frankie sprinted down the passage, barely looking where he was going. The ground shook beneath his feet. *One fall and I'll be a human pancake.*

But the passage seemed to go on forever. Frankie checked over his shoulder and saw the ball was picking up speed. He saw Medhi just ahead of the boulder, throwing back panicked glances. Then Frankie stopped.

"Dead end!" he cried.

Frankie spotted dim light at the side of the tunnel. *Another passage.*

"In there!" Frankie pointed.

Louise skidded to a halt and jumped into the narrow gap. Charlie went after her, then Max. Frankie followed, squeezing his body through.

"Wait for me!" yelled Medhi. But he was too big. He couldn't fit. The ball kept coming and the robber looked terrified. "Don't leave me!" he begged.

Frankie grabbed Medhi's arm. With a tug, he heaved him through the gap just as the crushing boulder rolled past and slammed into the wall ahead. It blocked the passage completely.

"You saved my life!" said Medhi.

Frankie wiped the sweat out of his eyes and took in the chamber around them. It was a square, and a smoldering torch rested in a metal loop above the door they'd come through. The room was completely bare apart from another stone soccer ball in the center. Louise looked around. "We're trapped!" she said. "There's no way out."

Max did the same, sniffing. "She's right."

Frankie took the torch from the

wall and ran it along the walls, looking for a hidden doorway. Nothing. But as he lifted the torch to the far wall, he saw it wasn't bare like the others. It was covered in carved symbols in neat columns and rows.

"Hieroglyphs!" said Charlie, proudly. "What do they say?"

Medhi looked at his feet. "I'm afraid I can't read."

"There must be a way out," said Frankie. He touched the wall. It didn't feel as cold as he expected. "It's not stone," he said. He rapped it with his knuckles and heard a hollow sound. "Wood!"

"I'll get us out," said Medhi. "Let's throw the ball at the wall and smash through it. Stand back, everyone!"

"Are you sure this is a good idea?" began Louise.

Medhi picked up the ball, and at the same moment dust showered down from the ceiling.

Then the roof began to inch closer.

"What have you done now?" Max whined. "You've set off another trap."

Medhi hurled the ball at the wooden wall, but it didn't even make a dent.

The ceiling shifted again, pressing down.

It's going to crush us! thought Frankie.

Medhi picked up the ball and threw it again with the same effect.

"I think we need a Plan B," he said.

CHAPTER 5

Keep calm, Frankie told himself. He tried to ignore the ceiling edging ever closer as he peered at the hieroglyphs. But what hope did he have? He couldn't read them any better than the tomb robber who'd brought them there.

One line of symbols, right in the

center, caught his attention. They looked ancient, like the others, but somehow different. These three little drawings showed a man in various positions with a round object.

"He's playing soccer!" said Frankie.

Louise came to his side. "I think I know how to get out," she said. "You have to match the pictures!"

Frankie looked again. In the first picture, the figure was balancing the ball on his right foot. In the second, on his left. In the third, he was bent over, with the ball behind his head, resting on the back of his neck.

But with a stone ball . . . ?

"Better do something quick," said Charlie, pointing upward. The ceiling was six feet up and pressing farther down by the second.

Frankie snatched the ball off the ground and rolled it onto his right foot. It was so heavy he could hardly hold it. He flicked the ball up a fraction and tried to catch it on his left. It rolled off.

"No time to be nervous," said Max. "Come on, Frankie!"

Frankie brought the ball back onto his right foot. He tossed it to his left foot. This time he managed to cushion the ball. Almost right away his left leg started to tremble with the weight.

"Get on with it!" cried Medhi. He began to crouch as the ceiling touched his hair.

Then the torch went out, and everything went dark.

Frankie took a deep breath. He'd done the trick a hundred times with a normal ball, but never in the dark. *If I get it wrong, I'll crack my skull.* He grunted as he jerked his foot upward and then bent at the waist to stoop beneath the ball. He felt the ball land on the back of his neck and wobble. Frankie maneuvered for balance.

At the same moment, the wooden wall cracked open in the center, flooding the room with light. The ceiling kept descending.

"You did it!" shouted Louise.

Blinking, Frankie let the stone ball drop to the ground and followed the others as they barreled through toward the light.

As his vision cleared, Frankie gasped at the sight below.

They stood on a balcony, high above an enormous square chamber lined with stone seats, all sloped like the outside of the pyramid. A thin shaft of light came through a hole in the roof, casting a line of shadow across the arena. Two goals, marked with stone posts, stood at opposite ends. All around the outside of the field were figures of men and women in soccer poses — reaching, kicking, stretching. *Weird,* thought Frankie. All that was missing from each statue was the soccer ball.

"This wasn't in my history books," said Louise, mouth gaping.

"For the last time, will the challengers please step forward?" said a man far below, in the center of the arena. Though he wore long black robes, and his head was shaved to a shine, Frankie recognized the Ref. He had a whistle hanging around his neck. "Otherwise," he continued, "the match is forfeit and the Menacing Mummy wins."

"We're here!" called Frankie without even thinking. Everyone turned to face them, and boos rippled through the chamber.

"You guys aren't very popular!" said Medhi, ducking back out of sight. "See ya!"

"At last!" said the Ref. "And what do you call yourselves?"

"Frankie's Fantasy FC," cried Louise.

The boos and hisses intensified, echoing off the stone walls.

The Ref held out his hands toward a set of golden doors behind him. "And where are our champions?" he bellowed.

The crowd all shot to their feet at once, and began to chant "KING TUT! KING TUT! KING TUT!"

Through the gateway came the boy Frankie had seen before. His sister with the straight bangs was trying to walk beside him, but he kept skipping in front, as if he wanted to lead the way. They pushed and pulled at each other as they entered the arena.

But behind them came something

that made Frankie's skin crawl. A giant snake slithered across the sandy ground. Its mouth was big enough to swallow Max.

"Something tells me that *thing* is on their team," said Max.

The snake had a rope tied over its neck and it dragged something very familiar: a huge oblong coffin, painted in bright colors and gold leaf.

"It's the sarcopha-thingy from the museum!" said Charlie.

The Ref edged cautiously toward the coffin and unfastened two clasps on the side. Crouching down, he pushed the lid open with a creak. Frankie, along with everyone else in the arena, found himself leaning forward. Inside the coffin lay a figure wrapped in bandages, completely still.

"It's the mummy!" whispered Louise.

The Ref stepped back, quaking. "Arise!" he called.

For a moment, nothing happened, and then the sound of a huge yawn came from the coffin. The mummy lifted one bandaged arm and gripped the side.

He sat up slowly.

"He's alive!" said Max.

"That's impossible," said Louise.

As the mummy raised a leg to climb out, he almost tripped. Tut ran

forward and gave him an arm to lean on.

"Steady, Dad," he said. "You've had a long nap."

"Let's go," said Frankie. He led the way down steep stone steps until they reached the bottom. The mummy turned stiffly to face them.

So did the snake. It opened its jaws wide to reveal long, dripping fangs.

"Theeee*ssse* mu*sss*t be our opponent*sss*," it hissed.

King Tut puffed out his chest. "Shouldn't be a problem," he said.

Princess Cleo sneered, and the mummy let out a long moan. The crowd responded with a cheer.

The Ref reached into the open sarcophagus and took out a golden mask and a golden soccer ball. "The winner will take the mummy's mask!" he said, placing it carefully on top of the coffin lid.

That must be what Medhi wanted to steal, thought Frankie. *It certainly looks like it's worth a lot of money.*

The Ref pointed to the shadow that moved slowly across the floor. "And the game will end when the shadow has crossed the field!" He brought his whistle to his lips.

"Ready?" Frankie said to his team.

Charlie and Louise nodded. Max wagged his tail.

The Ref blew the whistle and tossed the ball high into the air.

CHAPTER 6

Frankie ran for the ball, but so did King Tut. Frankie sprinted as fast as he could and got there a fraction before his opponent. He passed the ball out toward Louise. Cleo leapt from nowhere and blocked the pass.

"To me!" yelled her brother, hopping up and down. "Give it to me!"

Cleo ignored him and ran toward Charlie's goal. Frankie could see she was lightning fast. Max tried to tackle her, but she dribbled past him.

"I want it!" cried Tut.

But Cleo wasn't giving the ball to anyone. Frankie ran toward her, keeping his eyes on the ball. Max was chasing her, too. Cleo raised her foot to shoot . . .

Frankie slid across the ground, and knocked the ball away. Cleo ended up in a heap on the sandy ground.

"Why didn't you pass?" said her brother. He looked at the mummy.

"Dad! Tell her she shouldn't hog the ball."

The mummy groaned.

Frankie controlled the ball and kicked a short pass to Louise. "Let's stay close," he said. "That girl, Cleo, is quick."

Louise knocked the ball to Max. "Sure thing, Frankie."

As the dog turned, he came face-to-face with Viper, the snake. His eyes gleamed like black glass. "What's*sss* thi*sss* ta*sss*ty mor*sss*el?" he said.

Max skidded to a halt.

"Better watch out for Viper's

venom," said Tut. "It turns people to stone."

Frankie gulped, looking around at the statues at the edge of the arena. *So they're not statues after all,* he thought. *They're ex-players!*

Max backed off and then dug his front paws beneath the ball. He chipped it over the snake's head and scampered around him.

Quick as a flash, Viper twisted around and stopped the ball with his tail, balancing it right on the tip. Then he flicked it in a loop right to the mummy's feet.

The mummy groaned.

"Doesn't say much, does he?" said Louise.

"He never did," said Tut, his face sulky. "All he did when he was alive was play soccer. And when he wasn't playing, he liked to watch soccer."

"Sounds like my dad," said Charlie. "He's glued to the sports channel on the weekends."

The mummy moved slowly, wrapped in bandages.

I'll tackle him, no problem, Frankie thought.

But as he got closer, the mummy's feet became a blur of dummies and step-overs. Frankie tried to kick the ball, but he missed time and again.

"Go, Dad!" said Cleo. "Show them how it's done!"

The mummy blasted a shot at the goal, and Charlie dived low. He must have gotten a fingertip on the ball, because the shot bounced against the post and out again to Louise.

"Great save, Charlie!" said Frankie.

He noticed the shadow was moving quickly across the ground. It wouldn't be long until the game was over. Frankie had learned none of these matches were normal.

"Quick, Charlie!" said Frankie.

The goalie rolled the ball out to Frankie, who quickly turned and tried to run around the lumbering mummy.

But the bandaged figure quickly side stepped, blocking him. He tried the other way, but the mummy was there again. *It's like he can read my mind*, thought Frankie.

The arena was almost all in shadow. Frankie backheeled the ball to Louise. He realized too late that Viper had seen the pass. It reared back, fangs dripping, but Louise hadn't seen it.

"Look out!" Frankie yelled.

Louise turned and saw the snake darting its head at her, but she seemed glued to the spot. Then Charlie appeared, leaping through the air. Venom shot from Viper's

fangs, straight into Charlie's gloves. Right away, they thumped to the ground and turned to stone. Charlie ripped his hands free.

"You saved me!" said Louise.

"Always ready," gasped Charlie, blushing. "But what about my gloves?"

"What about the open goal?" Max barked.

The ball had rolled free. Both King Tut and Cleo dashed toward it.

Frankie sprinted forward, too.

"It's mine!" yelled the boy.

"No, it's *mine*!" snapped Cleo.

The mummy groaned, as if he was fed up with their squabbling. Quick as a flash, he shouldered Frankie aside and pounced on the ball and started to run at the goal. One of his bandages was trailing free.

Frankie watched in helpless horror as the mummy lifted his foot to shoot.

Then he stopped dead, snagged by his bandage. His foot swung through the empty air and he landed on his backside with a *thump*.

Frankie looked back and saw the other end of the bandage in Max's teeth. There was just a sliver of sunlight left. Frankie darted toward the ball, took a quick glance at the distant goal, and booted it as hard as he could.

As the ball arced across the arena, the crowd drew a deep breath. Frankie saw the Referee bringing the whistle toward his lips.

The ball landed right between the posts and bounced over the line.

PEEEEP!

The whistle blew and a second later Frankie felt Charlie leap onto his back.

"SUPERGOOAALL!" he cried. Frankie fell to his knees and Louise piled on, too. Max nudged his nose into the pileup, yapping happily.

CHAPTER 7

"Frankie's team is the winner!" said the Ref.

Cleo stamped her foot and crossed her arms. "What did I tell you?" she said to her brother. "*I* should have been captain, not you! Girls always make better leaders."

"If you passed the ball more often, we might have stood a chance!" said Tut.

The mummy groaned and started to shuffle back to his sarcophagus.

"He's probably fed up with listening to you two," said Louise.

"And now for the prize!" said the Ref. "Wait a minute . . . Where is it?"

Everyone looked to where the mask had been. It was gone!

"Someone's stolen it!" said the Ref.

Frankie glanced around and saw a man in the front row making for the steps. "Max!" he said, pointing. "Fetch!"

Max's ears pricked up and he dashed after the fleeing figure, fastening his teeth on the hem of his robe. With a ripping sound, it tore free.

Medhi, dressed in just his tunic, had the golden mask tucked into his belt.

"Ah . . . um . . . I can explain . . ."

The crowd began to boo as the two burly guards from outside gripped him by the shoulders.

"We need someone to help build a new pyramid," one said. "It should only take you twenty or thirty years."

As one of the guards dragged him away, Medhi cried out, "You don't

understand! I wasn't *stealing* it. I was looking after it. Safekeeping. You can't be too careful with all these thieves around . . ."

His voice trailed off as he disappeared through a door.

The other guard handed the mask back to Frankie, lowering his eyes. "Sorry we didn't believe you were the away team," he said.

"Don't worry," said Frankie, turning over the heavy mask in his hands. It was beautifully molded, with two holes for eyes. "We've had a fun adventure getting here."

"We almost got squashed twice!" mumbled Charlie. "You call that fun?"

Louise gave him an elbow in the ribs and he went quiet.

"Put the mask on, Frankie," she said.

"Why?" he asked.

"It's just a hunch I've got," she replied.

Frankie lifted the mask to his face and placed it against his skin. The gold was warm, and as soon as it touched his skin, his body felt weightless, like he was floating off the ground. Then, through the eyeholes, he saw he *was* floating off the ground. So were the others. Charlie wheeled his hands in panic, and Max's paws scrabbled in the air.

Louise grinned. "I think we're going home," she said.

Faster and faster they rose through the air, high above the Ref and the crowd. Wind whistled in Frankie's ears as they shot toward the ceiling.

"We're not going to stop!" he yelled.

Have I made a terrible mistake?

He raised his hands to shield himself and closed his eyes.

BOOM!

Frankie felt solid ground under his feet and he swayed dizzily.

He opened his eyes and saw the Egyptian room at the museum.

Charlie and Louise stood beside him. He was holding his magic soccer ball.

"You three!" bellowed a voice. They all spun around. Mr. Donald stood in the doorway, smoke practically shooting from his ears. Beside him stood a woman with a museum name tag. "Ms. Jones here told me there were children playing soccer in the museum," said their teacher. "Explain yourselves."

Frankie looked at the ball in his hands, then at Charlie and Louise. Charlie shrugged — he was wearing his gloves again, and they weren't made of stone. Louise opened her mouth as if she was about to speak, then closed it again.

What can I possibly say?

"As I thought," said Mr. Donald. "You three will be in detention next week. I might even have to call your . . ."

"Oh my!" gasped Ms. Jones. She ran from Mr. Donald's side, straight past Frankie, and stopped at the rope beside the sarcophagus. "It . . . it can't be!"

Frankie drew a sharp breath. The coffin wasn't empty anymore. Inside stood the golden mask, gleaming brightly.

"The mummy's mask!" said the museum worker. "But how . . . ? It's never been found!"

"I guess it has now," said Frankie.

Mr. Donald had come in as well, and he was gaping at the mask.

Charlie leaned close to Frankie's

ear. "I think Donaldo's forgotten about detention," he whispered. "Maybe we should get back to the bus."

"Good idea!" said Frankie.

ACKNOWLEDGMENTS

Many thanks to everyone at Little, Brown Book Group UK; Neil Blair, Zoe King, Daniel Teweles, and all at The Blair Partnership; Mike Jackson for bringing my characters to life; special thanks to Michael Ford for all his wisdom and patience; and to Steve Kutner for being a great friend and for all his help and guidance not just with this book but with everything.

CHECK OUT FRANKIE AND HIS FRIENDS' FIRST ADVENTURE:

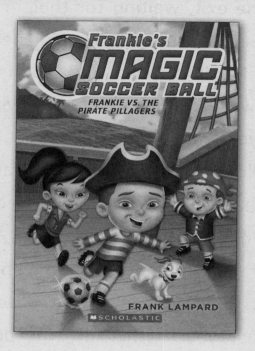

"Should we go in, too?" Frankie asked. "Maybe Louise got lost."

"Nah," said Charlie, glancing toward the haunted house. "She'll be out soon."

Frankie and Charlie were standing by the exit, waiting for their friend Louise. The sun was dropping behind the Ferris wheel, and soon the carnival would be shutting down for the year and leaving town.

"Not scared, are you?" said Frankie.

Charlie blushed, and all his freckles stood out. "Of course not."

Frankie grinned. He remembered that Charlie hadn't wanted to go in last year, either. It *was* pretty scary. There were walking skeletons, dangling spiders, and wailing ghosts. He would have gone in again today with Louise, but it cost a dollar and he only had fifty cents left.

Frankie's dog, Max, was sniffing around the ground looking for scraps of food.

"Here you go, boy," Frankie said. He reached into his pocket and pulled out a dog biscuit. Max opened his mouth and Frankie dropped it in, then tickled the dog under his furry white muzzle.

The doors opened and a few screams drifted over. Then a balding man with pale skin and wide eyes stumbled out. It was their gym teacher, Mr. Donald.

"Looks like Donaldo's spooked," said Frankie.

Mr. Donald saw them and walked

over, smoothing down the few hairs on his head.

"Is that a spider on your shoulder, sir?" asked Charlie.

Mr. Donald jumped about a foot in the air, craning his neck.

"Only joking, sir," said Charlie.

Mr. Donald stared at them with a frown. "I hope to see you both at soccer practice tomorrow."

"Of course, sir," said Frankie. "We wouldn't miss practice for anything!"

Mr. Donald walked off, still checking his shoulder.